*Because of Kamtza and Bar Kamtza,
Jerusalem was destroyed.*

Babylonian Talmud, Tractate Gittin 55b

For Yotam and for Yuval.

Green
Bean
Books

First published in Hebrew in 2019 by Am Oved, Israel.
First published in English in 2021 by Green Bean Books,
c/o Pen & Sword Books Ltd
47 Church Street, Barnsley, South Yorkshire, S70 2AS, England
www.greenbeanbooks.com

With special thanks to Shira Atik who translated the text for the English
edition and to Batnadiv HaKarmi for her help in translating pages 20–21.

Edited by Kate Baker and Phoebe Jascourt
Production by Hugh Allan

Printed in China by 1010 Printing International Ltd
012131.2K1/B1614/A7

MIX
Paper from
responsible sources
FSC® C016973

Lenny and Benny

Naama Benziman

The story of Kamtza and Bar Kamtza is
set in the days before the destruction of
the Second Temple in Jerusalem. It is a
story filled with conflict. This is a *very*
different version of that tale . . .

Lenny lived in a small house at the edge of a forest. Every morning, he would drink his cocoa, water his rosebush, and then head off to practice his jumping.

Lenny was training for a competition.

Loppity Lop!

Loppity Lop!

FOREST JUMPING

In the first race,
he beat the flea.

In the second race,
he beat the flea and the frog.

In the third race,
he beat the flea, the frog,
and the squirrel.

And that's how he became . . .

THE JUMPING CHAMPION

OF THE FOREST

LENNY

Jumpity Jump!

One day, Benny showed up from the other edge of the forest.

Lenny invited Benny to his house. They drank cocoa. They nibbled on cookies. They had the best day *ever!*

"But now," Lenny said,
"I have to go and practice."
"Practice what?" Benny asked.
"Jumping," replied Lenny.
"Haven't you heard?
I'm the Jumping Champion of the Forest!"
"Can I practice, too?" Benny asked.
Eager to help Benny learn how to jump,
Lenny agreed.
So they started jumping together.

Loppity... But wait... How can this be? Is he beating me?

Jumpity Jump!

You're a cheater!!!
I saw you cheat!
You didn't start at the right place!

You're a liar!
I'll never play with you again!
Go away and don't you
ever come back!
I'm not your friend
anymore!
You're a liar-cheat!
The king of liars
and the king of cheaters!!!
You're the biggest liar-cheat
and the trickiest trickster
and the biggest bluffer in the
whole wide world!

The next day, Benny sent a drawing to Lenny.
Lenny opened up the envelope, crumpled the
picture, and threw it on the floor.

A week later, Benny sent a new drawing to Lenny.
This time Lenny didn't even open the envelope.

A month later, Benny sent yet another drawing to Lenny.
"I don't want any drawings made by liars!" Lenny shouted.
"I'm not friends with liars! I'm not talking to Benny, and I'll
never talk to him again, not now, not ever!"

And he tore it all up into teeny-tiny pieces.

BENNY'S PARTY

Benny's birthday was
at the beginning of summer.

He prepared a super-awesome party,
with long, stretchy candy, chocolate lollipops,
and popsicles in every color. He sent
beautiful invitations to all the forest
animals . . . except for Lenny.

But the postman accidentally put
an invitation in Lenny's mailbox.

Lenny was surprised to get the invitation.

"Wow! What a super-awesome party!"
he thought to himself.
"I guess Benny really wants us to make up.
I suppose the jumping incident was a
very long time ago now, and I would surely
beat him by a landslide if we tried again."

Lenny thought about it for a minute.
"In honor of Benny's birthday, I've decided
we should be friends again."

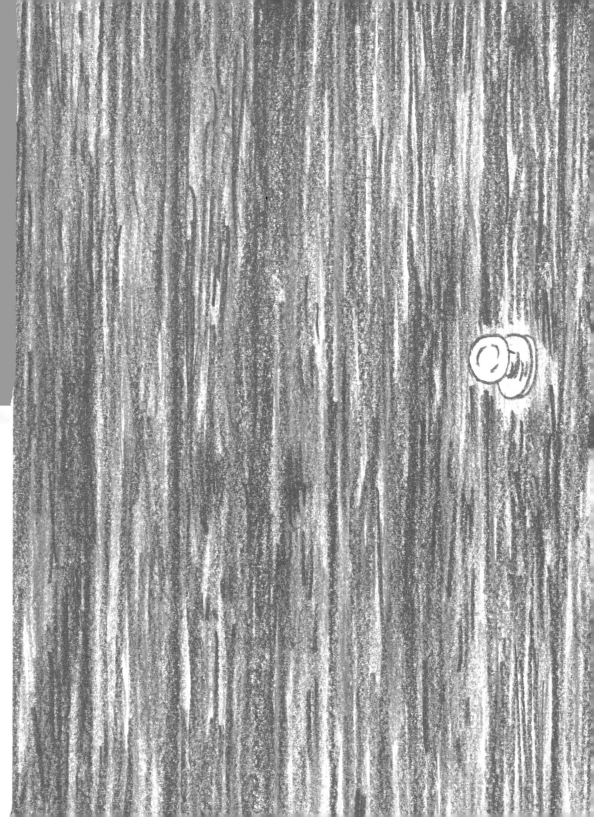

When Lenny arrived, all the other
guests were already sitting around
the big party table.

Benny looked at Lenny in surprise.
"What are *you* doing here?!"

Loppity Lop!

Loppity Lop!

BENNY'S
PARTY

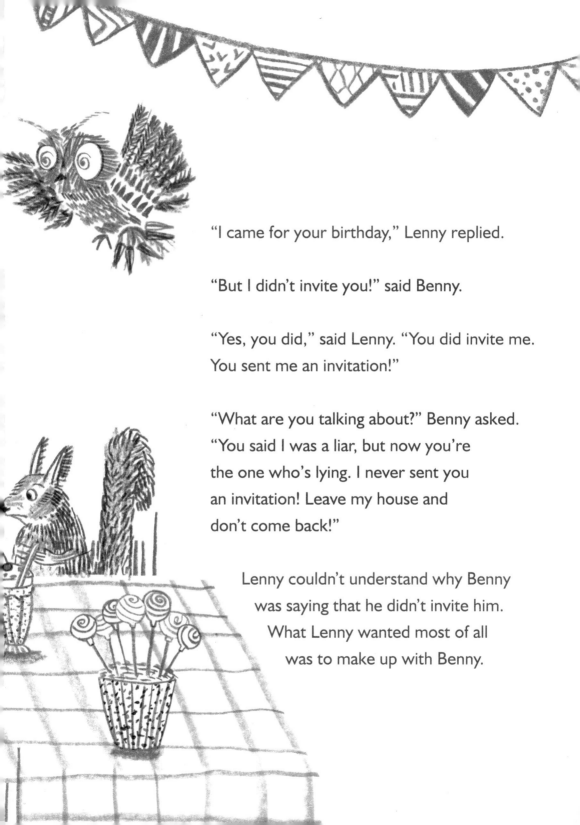

"I came for your birthday," Lenny replied.

"But I didn't invite you!" said Benny.

"Yes, you did," said Lenny. "You did invite me. You sent me an invitation!"

"What are you talking about?" Benny asked. "You said I was a liar, but now you're the one who's lying. I never sent you an invitation! Leave my house and don't come back!"

Lenny couldn't understand why Benny was saying that he didn't invite him. What Lenny wanted most of all was to make up with Benny.

let me stay. I'll show you my invitation tomorrow. I really want us to be friends again.

Please, Benny, please

Please, Benny, I'll help you with the whole party, and I'll do whatever you want!

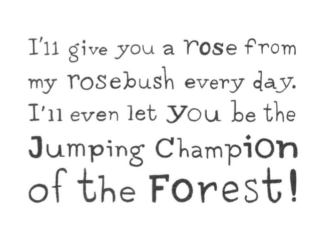

I'll give you a rose from my rosebush every day. I'll even let you be the Jumping Champion of the Forest!

NO! NO! NO! NO!

I'll **never** talk to you again, not now, not **ever**!

Soon the summer was over.
Autumn passed and
winter arrived.

Then one day, when the snow started melting,
Benny saw the present from Lenny sitting outside
his house. On top of the gift was a beautiful
drawing that Lenny had made. Benny smiled
down at the picture, remembering how they'd
had the best day ever.

Loppity Lop!

Jumpity Jump!

Dear Friend,

Now that you've read this book, you know how Lenny and Benny's story ends, but the original tale – which appears in the Talmud* – ends quite differently. It goes like this:

Sometime around the year 70 CE (which was a long time ago!), there was a man living in Jerusalem who decided to host a party. This man's best friend was named Kamtza, and the man's worst enemy was named Bar Kamtza. Of course, he decided to invite Kamtza to his party, but he never once thought of inviting Bar Kamtza. And what happened? The invitation was delivered to Bar Kamtza by mistake! Can you believe it?

Bar Kamtza was surprised and happy to be invited, but when he arrived at the party, the host behaved very badly.

"You are my enemy!" the host yelled. "Why are you here? Get out!"
"You invited me!" Bar Kamtza said. "Can I please stay? I'll pay for everything I eat and drink."
"No!" shouted the host.
"I'll pay for half of the party," Bar Kamtza pleaded.
"No!"
"I'll pay for the whole party!"
"No! You have to go! Now!"

*The Talmud is the core collection of rabbinic writings.

The other guests, some of whom were leaders in the community, watched all of this happen, but no one spoke up for Bar Kamtza. They stood silently as the host threw him out.

Bar Kamtza was angry and hurt. Who wouldn't be? He decided to take revenge against everyone who had been at the party. He spread rumours about the host and guests. His words found their way to the Roman emperor, who ruled Jerusalem at the time. The emperor reacted by sending an army to destroy the Second Temple of Jerusalem and exiling the Jewish people from their country. It was a catastrophe that changed the course of Jewish history.

All of that happened because of a simple mistaken invitation to a party? That's right. According to the Talmud, those terrible events can be traced to the story of Kamtza and Bar Kamtza.

It's okay to feel angry sometimes, but we can learn to control the way we react to our feelings. Hatred and meanness spread easily. Fortunately, kindness and forgiveness can spread just as easily. Kamtza and Bar Kamtza show us what can happen in a community if hatred takes control. Lenny and Benny show us another option. We can, and we should, choose kindness instead.